This book was made especially for

CASSIDY

Dear Cassidy,

Words cannot express how special you are. But, here are twenty-six that try! Each one so perfectly describes you. You are all of these wonderful qualities— and so much more.

Love,

_____

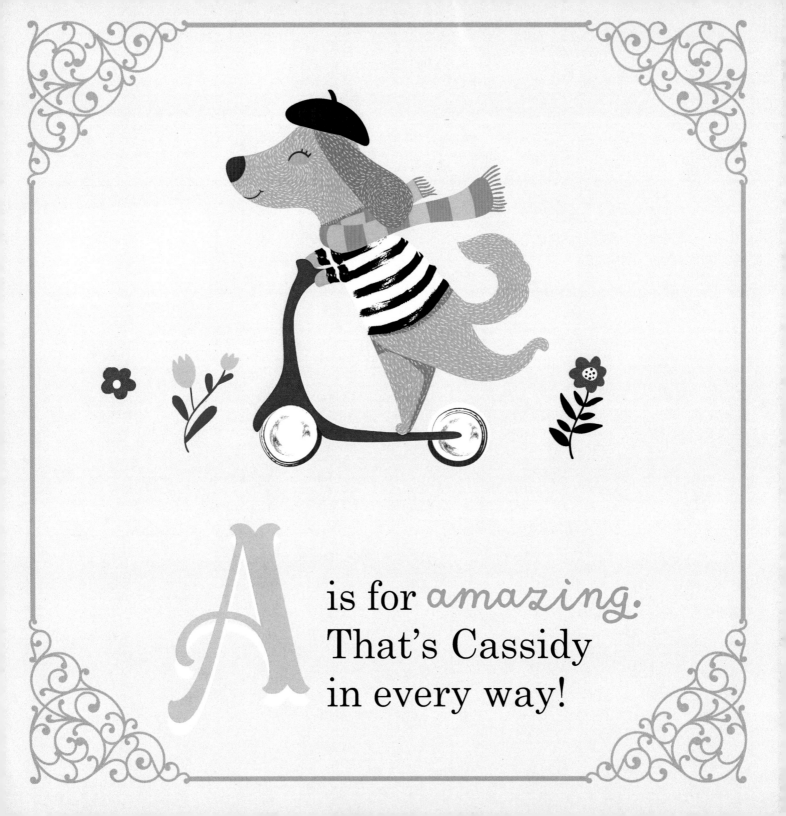

A is for *amazing.* That's Cassidy in every way!

B is for the special way you *brighten* up each day.

C is for your *courage*. You don't fear what to do.

D

is for your *daring*.
You always
carry through.

E is for your *energy*,
so vibrant and
so bright!

F is for the *fun*
you bring to all
both day and night.

G describes your future. Oh, the places you will *go!*

H is for the *heights* you'll climb and successes you will know.

I's *imagination* and the power of your dreams.

J is for the *joy* you bring, your shining face that beams.

K is for your *kindness*,
shown to big and small.

L is for the *love* you freely share with one and all.

M is for your *music*, the song of your own heart.

N is meant for *never,*
for we'll never,
ever part.

O means there is *one* you—there never will be two!

P is meant for *perfect*—it's you just being you.

Q is all the *qualities*
I notice every time.

R is how you're *rare*, like a diamond from a mine.

S is meant for *super,*
for you have pow'r
to soar!

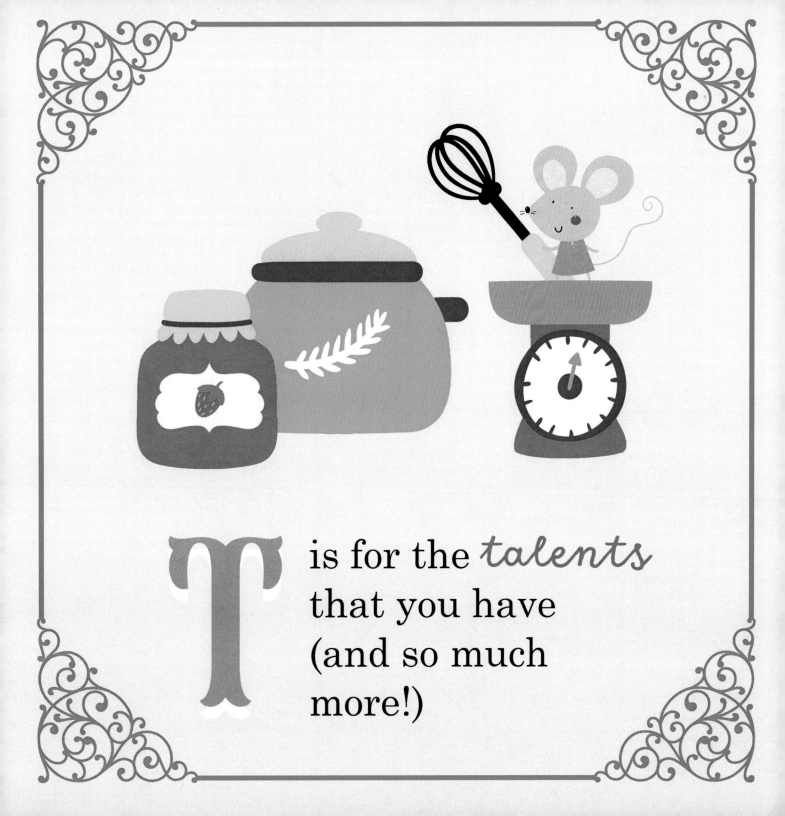

T is for the *talents* that you have (and so much more!)

U is for *unique* in every bold sense of the word.

V is for your *voice*.
Don't be afraid
that you'll
be heard!

W is for *wild.*
Always live and
gallop free!

X

is xceptional,
xtraordinarily!

YOU

Y is meant for *you*,
the only one
there'll ever be.

But day is done, and you must sleep, so

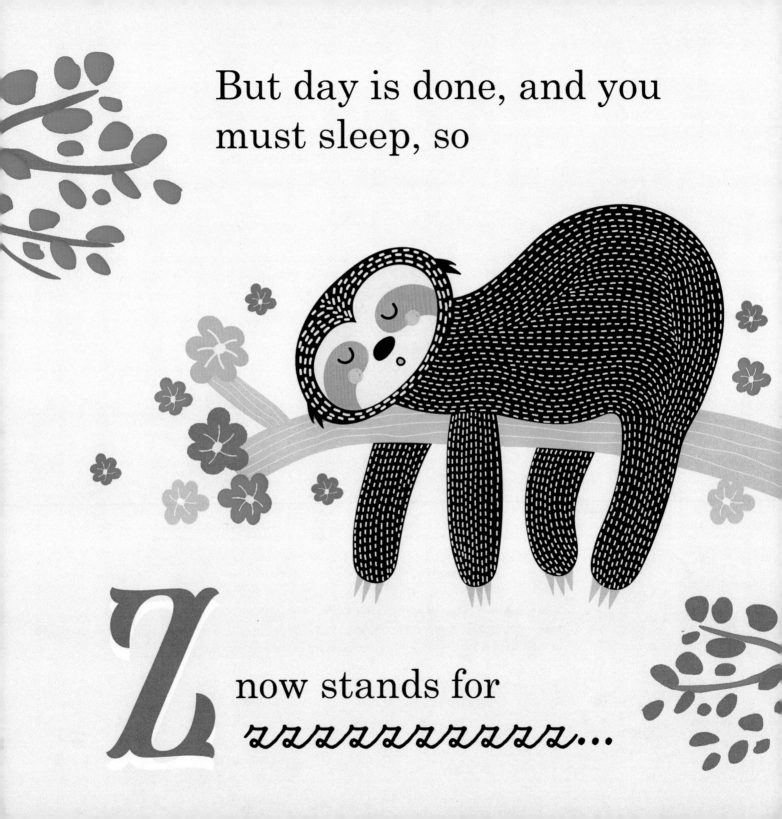

Z now stands for

zzzzzzzzzzzzz...

Li'l Llama
CUSTOM KIDS BOOKS

Cover and book design by David Miles

Visual credits: bear with umbrella, bear with ice cream, giraffe on bicycle, bear on bicycle, bear on unicycle, dog on scooter (StudioLondon/Shutterstock.com); boat (NadineVeresk/Shutterstock.com); sloth (jsabirova/Shutterstock.com); wave pattern (Vecteezy.com); dancing horse, llama, super dog, zebra, birds, dinosaur, deer, cat and dog, cat and bird, unicorn (lena_nikolaeva/Shutterstock.com); tree branches (Ardea-studio/Shutterstock.com); cloud pattern (love pattern/Shutterstock.com); bird tree branch (PinkPueblo/Shutterstock.com); mouse (Nadezda Barkova/Shutterstock.com); cooking items, space elements (Beskova Ekaterina/Shutterstock.com); diamond (Olga_Angelloz/Shutterstock.com); leaf pattern (Mangata/Shutterstock.com); singing cat, astronaut mouse, monkey sailor (Maria Skrigan/Shutterstock.com); rabbits (Natasha_Chetkova/Shutterstock.com); village (ussr/Shutterstock.com); radial burst (HPLTW/Shutterstock.com); goat (Tartila/Shutterstock.com); mountains (LoveZ/Shutterstock.com); animals in hot air balloon (Maria Starus/Shutterstock.com); flowers (mejorana/Shutterstock.com); rainbow (fruestig/Shutterstock.com); sun (Nikolaeva/Shutterstock.com); spine pattern (Curly Pat/Shutterstock.com); page borders (Giraphics/Shutterstock.com); clouds (Marina_Che/Shutterstock.com); large rainbow (Peter Hermes Furian/Shutterstock.com); graph paper background (Vector Plus Image/Shutterstock.com).

Made in United States
North Haven, CT
10 June 2022

20095574R00018